The Three Little KITTENS Get Dressed

■ SCHOLASTIC

Children's Press®
A Division of Scholastic Inc.
New York Toronto London Auckland Sydney
Mexico City New Delhi Hong Kong Danbury, Connecticut

**Early Childhood
Consultants:**

Ellen Booth Church
Diane Ohanesian

1 2 3 4 5 6 7 8 9 10 R 19 18 17 16 15 14 13 12 11 10   62

Library of Congress Cataloging-in-Publication Data

The three little kittens get dressed.
    p. cm. – (Rookie preschool)
    Summary: While helping the forgetful feline trio find its missing mittens, the reader is introduced to other items of clothing suitable for playing outside on a cold and snowy day.
    ISBN-13: 978-0-531-24404-3 (lib. bdg.)   ISBN-13: 978-0-531-24579-8 (pbk.)
    ISBN-10: 0-531-24404-0   (lib. bdg.)   ISBN-10: 0-531-24579-9 (pbk.)

1. Stories in rhyme. 2. Clothing and dress—Fiction. 3. Lost and found possessions—Fictions. 4. Cats—Fiction. 5. Animals—Infancy—Fiction.   I. Title. II. Series

PZ8.3.T415 2010
[E] – dc22   2009005793

The three little kittens have lost their mittens.

Oh no! Where are our mittens?

They can't go out to play.

Let's help the kittens find their mittens

on this cold and snowy day.

Let's look for the mittens under the chair.

Could the mittens be hiding there?

No, the mittens are not
under the chair.

But there are three snuggly hats . . .

just right for three little cats!

Let's look for the mittens
under the bed.

Did someone put them there instead?

No, the mittens are not
under the bed.

But they find three sweaters,
red, green, and blue.

These will keep three kittens warm, too.

Let's look for the mittens under the stairs.

Make sure to look for three little pairs.

No, the mittens are not
under the stairs.

But there are three coats, warm as toast.

The kittens think they like them the most!

Let's look for the mittens
out in the hall.

Were they put on a shelf after all?

No, the mittens are not on a shelf.

But there were boots, all in a row...

just perfect for playing out in the snow!

The kittens hurry out in the snow.
They look in their pockets and—
what do you know?

The three little kittens found their mittens!

Rookie Storytime Tips

In this new twist on a favorite nursery rhyme, *The Three Little Kittens Get Dressed* takes your preschooler on a mitten hunt that helps the forgetful kittens dress for a snowy day. As you and your child share this book, invite comparisons of what the kittens wear with your child's own seasonal clothing. It's a great way to help him or her build awareness of dressing for the weather.

Invite your child to go back through the book and find the following. Along the way, you'll build visual discrimination and reinforce concepts of clothing and parts of the body.

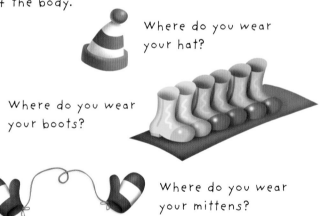

Where do you wear your hat?

Where do you wear your boots?

Where do you wear your mittens?

Look out the window. What would you wear to play outside today?